Dinosaur Christmas

by
Jerry Pallotta

Illustrated by
Howard McWilliam

SCHOLASTIC INC.
New York   Toronto   London   Auckland
Sydney   Mexico City   New Delhi   Hong Kong

A merry Christmas to Dr. Annekathryn Goodman.

—J.P.

For Rebecca, with love.

—H.M.

ISBN 978-0-545-24963-8

Text copyright © 2011 by Jerry Pallotta. Illustrations copyright © 2011 by Howard McWilliam.

12 11 10 9 8 7 6 5 4 3 2 1   11 12 13 14 15 16/0

Printed in Singapore   46

First Scholastic printing, November 2011

Reindeer are great at their jobs.

But I remember the good old days . . .

. . . when dinosaurs pulled my sleigh.

Triceratops were
steady and ready . . .
but a bit slow.

So I tried Parasaurolophus.

They tooted,
honked, and squeaked
too loud.

I tried Pterosaurs.
They flew so high.
Help! I couldn't breathe.

And those Velociraptors.

They were fidgety. *Stop slashing at each other!*

It was a gigantic-o
mistake-o!

And those Tyrannosaurus rex . . .

They wouldn't
stop licking me!

The Maiasauras were pretty and well behaved.

Until they ate the presents.
Bad dinosaurs!
I'm telling your mother!

Oh! And those Styracosaurus.

Pushy and *way* too bossy.

Then I tried
Stegosaurus.

It was a merry, spiky,
pointy Christmas.

I tried Gallimimus.

They wouldn't stop dancing.

The Apatosaurus
worked well.

They were great
for deliveries and
seeing ahead.

Ankylosaurus,
Zephyrosaurus,
Nodosaurus —
    they never bored us.

Today the dinosaurs are gone.

Now the reindeer are my helpers.
And they're a treasure.

But sometimes
I miss the
good old days.

Merry Christmas!